Deep Surrendering

To Kathy,

XOXO

CHELSEA M. CAMERON

Chapter One

Heartbreaker. That was the first word that came to mind when I met Fintan Herald. The second word was tall. If he were to kiss me—something I thought completely improbable at the time—he would have to bend in half to get our lips to meet. Or I'd have to use a ladder. But then he looked at me with eyes that were like sapphires, and I forgot about him being anything other than stunningly attractive. The crazy part was, he seemed to be interested in me, too.

I thought he was crazy for my friend Rory. After all, their parents had matched them up since birth. They had an easy relationship that made my heart sink. But after exchanging a few words, he'd turned to me and said, "Well, Marisol Everly. Tell me about yourself."

Even in the dark of the bar, I could see his eyes glowing, and that his full attention was on me. Our first conversation hadn't been anything memorable like in the movies. I'd talked about my graduate classes, he'd talked about his job, and then he'd given me his number.

Nothing about it had been special, but when I got home, all I could think about was Fin. His eyes, his hands, his glorious hair, and the way he could block out all the chaos of the bar to listen to me drone on about my classes. Nothing about me was riveting, but still. He wanted to see me again.

"I don't care what you say, how many times have I told you that if you were on my team, I would have gone for you the first time I met you?" Chloe said the next morning as we had brunch. She'd gotten a little bit drunk the night before (I'd been mildly tipsy), so her usual hangover breakfast of lobster eggs Benedict was in order.

"I know, Chlo. I've heard it," I said, rolling my eyes and sipping my orange juice. In my relationship with Chloe, I was the moderate one. The cautious one. She'd say the boring one.

"So why can't you accept the fact that some guy would see how incredibly awesome you are? He'd be a moron not to." Like a true best friend, Chloe was the captain of Team Marisol.

"I know, I know," I said, rolling my eyes. Chloe glared at me.

"So, do you like him?"

What wasn't to like? If I wrote a list of top qualities I'd want in a man, Fin had all of them, plus bonus points.

"I barely know him." A few hours with someone didn't make a relationship. It might have gone against the grain to not jump right into bed with a guy after barely a hello, but I guessed I was just old-fashioned that way. Chloe was always telling me my standards were too high and that all my rules were just an excuse not to get close to someone. She was probably right, but that didn't mean I was going to change my dating policy overnight.

"There are a lot of ways to get to know someone. One of those ways is by getting naked. You can learn a lot about someone by having sex with them." I was sure you could. It seemed to have worked for Rory.

But there was another reason Chloe was concentrating on my relationship instead trying to find her own. Harmony had completely destroyed her. I'd seen it coming from miles away, but I didn't want to

upset Chloe. When it ended, I couldn't say I knew it was going to happen, I could only offer my shoulder and tell her that I was on the lookout for eligible lesbians.

At the talk of sex, Chloe stared off into space, and I knew she was thinking about Harmony again. Those moments had become few and far between, but they still happened now and then.

Not that she was going to get over Harmony with a snap of the fingers and some rebound sex, and that was as it should be. You didn't get over someone you loved that quickly.

"You okay?" I asked. It seemed to break her out of it. She shook her head and then tucked her hair behind her ears.

"Yeah, sorry. I'm back." She gave me a tight smile and I reached out to rub her arm. "It's just because I'm hung over," she said, resting her head on the table.

"It's okay, sweetie. You *will* get through this. You're the strong one."

"You mean I'm the bitch," she said, raising her head and wiping her eyes with one hand.

I pretended not to see her tears. I was about to say something else, but then my phone buzzed with a new text message.

"I will bet you ten thousand dollars that text is from Fin," Chloe said, her mood going from depressed and bitter to excited at the prospect a boy might have texted me.

"As a matter of fact it is," I said, picking up the phone and scanning the message quickly. That was fast. I wasn't expecting him to contact me this soon. Wasn't there something about a three-day rule for communication after a date? But last night wasn't technically a date, so maybe that was why he texted me only a few hours after we'd last seen each other. It was only three words, but those words still made my heart flutter.

Good morning, Marisol.

It was a simple, seemingly sterile text, but I could hear his voice saying it to me with a little bit of a smile playing on his face. I had no idea what to say to him, and I didn't want to sound to eager, so I went for formal.

Good morning, Fin. How are you? I texted back.

"You definitely like him. You're smiling as you're texting him. That is definitely a sign. So, what does Mr. Fin have to say?" I shook my head and waited for his response.

I'm doing well, Marisol. I was just thinking that maybe I'd like to see you again.

I couldn't help the little leap of excitement in my stomach when I read those words. I wanted to see him, too.

"What is he saying?" Chloe reached out and got a hold of my phone, and read our text exchange. "Oh, babe. He wants you. You'd better not say no." I had no intention of saying no. Well, to the date. I would definitely say no to anything more. I could say no to Fin. I would say no to Fin.

I would try to say no to Fin.

Chapter
Two

"So what are we doing today?" I asked as Fin opened the door of a rented black Town Car, complete with driver. Tres fancy. I was glad I'd worn one of my nicer dresses and favorite boots, even though Fin had been very cryptic about what we were doing. Spontaneity was sexy, and so was he.

He got in next to me and shut the door with a wink.

"The Prudential Center, please Carl."

"Right away, Sir," Carl said. He was even wearing one of those chauffeur hats. It gave me flashbacks to my childhood when my mother had a driver. I definitely didn't want to think about my mother, so I sat back on the leather seats and tried to figure out what we could be doing at the Prudential Center. There were lots of shops and restaurants, but it was the middle of the afternoon. Too late for lunch and too early for dinner.

"You're not going to tell me what we're doing, are you?" I said as Fin stared out the window. He turned to me with a smile.

"You'll see," he said, and slid closer to me, the leather of the seat creaking. "And can I say that you look stunning today?"

"You can. I'm not going to stop you." I knew I was grinning like a schoolgirl, but I couldn't help it. It had been a long time since I'd felt such sweet flutters in my stomach. Being with Fin was like having a high school crush, when every glance cast your way set you on fire.

"You look pretty good yourself, sir." He did, in a crisp green shirt and dark jeans with a set of boots that looked like they were much loved, judging by the scuffmarks. I liked that. Most of his clothes looked fresh from the cleaners, but those boots were worn-in.

"Why thank you." We lapsed into silence as Carl navigated the snarly Boston traffic. I hadn't grown up here, but I'd adopted the city and it felt like home now. Even after living here for years, there were still nooks and crannies I hadn't yet explored.

Fin was quiet until we pulled up in front of the Prudential Center, but he smiled as he held the door open for me and thanked Carl. I wondered what he was going to do to occupy himself while we were doing whatever we were doing. I hoped he at least had a book or something.

"Ready?" Fin asked, holding his hand out.

"Sure," I said, taking it and feeling a spark go up my arm as my skin touched his. I had no idea what I was ready for, but it didn't really matter.

"Did you know that I was born in Boston but I have never taken a Duck Tour?" Fin said as one of the famous Boston Duck Boats pulled up in front of us. I'd understood when we didn't go inside the

Prudential Center that it wasn't our final destination. Just a starting place.

"I haven't either," I said. It was one of those things that I always told myself I'd do but never followed through on.

I looked at the purple-painted contraption idling in front of us.

"This is it? We're doing a Duck Tour?" I asked just to make sure.

He nodded. "And then dinner, if the tour goes well. If it doesn't go well, then I'll have Carl drop you back at your apartment. But I'm hoping it will go well." He squeezed my hand and led me toward the boat-slash-bus. Long and open-air, it looked nothing like a duck, but the name referred to its ability to go from land to water.

It was empty.

"I, uh, booked a private tour. Hope that's okay." I didn't know what to say to that. The expense of renting it out was probably nothing to him, but as a grad student, that would have bought nearly all my textbooks for a semester.

"It's great," I said as he led me up the steps and the tour guide greeted us. We sat in the very front seat and Fin put his arm around me.

"I'm really glad you're here with me," he said. "I feel like when I travel so much I never get to actually see anything. That's what I'm going to do, wherever I go."

"How many places have you been?" His hand started making its way up and down my arm as the Duck Boat turned into traffic and the tour guide started talking.

Fin didn't answer for a little while, and I thought maybe he hadn't heard me, or he was just interested in the little-known facts of Boston.

"I don't even know, Marisol. I've forgotten. It's all blended together in a haze of hotel rooms and conference rooms and meetings and suits and ties." He shook his head, and for the first time, he looked downcast.

"So what are you going to do about it?" He pulled me closer as we barreled through the streets.

"I'm going to pay attention to the things that matter. Like this." His hand went under my chin and pulled my face up. "I'm going to pay attention to you and the way the sun catches the darker streaks in your hair, the pink in your cheeks, and your beautiful eyes. That's what I'm going to pay attention to. Right here, right now."

I nearly melted off my seat.

"But you don't even know me," I said. This was too much, too fast. Even though I'd been hearing about him from Rory, I still didn't really know what mattered. The important things. Life was all about the little details.

Like if he was a morning person, what his favorite breakfast cereal was, what song always got stuck in his head, how his relationship was with his mother.

He shrugged one shoulder and pulled my face closer.

"I know that right now I'm paying very close attention to your lips, and I'd like to pay even closer attention to them." I turned my head at the last moment so he missed and got my cheek.

"I'm sorry," I said, hoping he wouldn't hate me. "I have a no-kiss-on-the-first-date rule." It sounded even worse out loud. I sounded like some sort of stick-up-her-ass prude.

"No kiss on the first date?" Fin said, turning his head to the side as if he was fascinated by me.

"Is that a problem?" God, I hoped not.

He grinned at me and flicked my hair over my shoulder.

"Not at all," he said, but then he started laughing.

"And what's so funny?" He shook his head, his shoulders shaking. "Hey. What is so damn funny?" I poked him in the chest.

"Ow!" Now I was laughing as he rubbed the place on his chest where I'd poked him.

"Shh. You're being rude to the tour guide," I said, turning away from him and focusing back on the fellow driving our Duck Boat who didn't seem upset in the slightest that we'd been ignoring him. He could probably do his spiel in his sleep, sans audience.

"In 2010, these vehicles were used to transport flood victims in Wayland, Massachusetts to safety," the guide said.

"Did you know that in 2010 these vehicles were used to transport flood victims in Wayland to safety?" Fin said, parroting the tour guide.

"No, I did not know that. Thank you for sharing that fact with me, Fin Herald." I was glad to have a distraction from the kiss conversation. I couldn't tell how he felt about it, but he didn't try to kiss me again the whole rest of the tour.

I tried not to scream when we splashed into the water but failed, and Fin held me close. The sun danced off the water, and the harbor bustled with traffic, just like the city streets.

"It's so beautiful out here," I said, leaning against Fin as we chugged along. "Are you paying attention to this?" I pointed at the city around us.

"I'm trying to. You're very distracting."

"How am I distracting? I'm not doing anything." Well, I was blushing now.

"How long have you two been together?" asked the tour guide, interrupting what Fin might have said.

"This is our first date, actually," I said.

"And how's it going so far?" he said with a grin. I let Fin answer that one.

"Best first date ever," he said, squeezing my shoulder.

"Aw, give her a kiss now. Come on!" I couldn't get out of it now. Fin turned to me.

"We have to do what the man says. He might make us walk the plank if we don't. How about it?" I had willpower. I had standards that

I'd lived up to (for the most part), but all of those things vaporized when Fin smiled at me and cocked one eyebrow.

"What the hell," I said, and puckered my lips, hoping he would get the hint and just give me a quick peck.

It was the briefest of brief kisses. Before I knew it was happening, it was over.

"There. That wasn't so bad, was it?" Fin asked, licking his bottom lip. No, it wasn't bad. It was just…it was too quick to judge. I needed a second opinion. If we counted last night as a date, then this was technically our second date, and completely in the realm of kiss territory.

"I'm not sure. I think we need to try it again. Later, though. Maybe at the end of the night." His face broke into a smile.

"What about the no kiss rule?"

I shrugged one shoulder. "Screw it. We'll call this the second date."

"Well you know what they say about the third date." There was a devilish twinkle in his eye.

"I have no idea what you're talking about," I said, even though I knew perfectly well that the rule was that you put out on the third date. Fin leaned close, and I thought he was going to kiss my ear, but he spoke instead.

"They say that on the third date, the girl has to…receive flowers." He chuckled and his breath on my neck made me shiver. I turned my head to see if he was kidding.

"What kind of flowers?"

"Whatever are her favorite." I tapped my chin, pretending to think on that.

"Most girls would probably say roses."

He nodded. "That's true. Most girls would. But I'm inquiring about one particular girl."

"Oh, in that case…. Lilacs. Either purple or white. My grandmother had a row of them outside her house and we'd sit in the garden and have tea parties and she'd read to me. When I smell them, it's like traveling back in time, and I can see her face and hear her voice again." Fin looked at me for several minutes before he said anything. I'd probably said too much. I wasn't normally like this. There were things about me even Chloe didn't know.

"Lilacs it is," he finally said.

Chapter
Three

Fin took me to an early dinner at a chic restaurant in the Prudential Center. One of those places with terrible lighting and tiny portions. It wouldn't have been my first choice, but I didn't want to make any waves.

"The chef here is supposed to be world class, but I'm not seeing anything that great on the menu," Fin said, his eyes skipping back and forth. I definitely didn't see anything I wanted and I wasn't a very picky eater.

"Oh?" I said, trying to gauge whether he was thinking of leaving, or if we'd stay anyway.

"Yeah. Do you see anything?" I looked around at the place. It was cold and impersonal. Sparse furnishings, poor lighting and oddly shaped chairs that looked like they'd hurt your back. It was supposed to be "modern," but it came off pretentious.

"Not really." Honesty was best, right?

He slapped the menu down on the table. "Then what are we doing here?" he asked, pushing his chair, standing and giving me his hand with a smile. "Come with me."

"Now this, this is perfect," I said twenty minutes later when we were sitting on a bench in the park, eating fish tacos purchased from one of the many food trucks that seemed to buzz around the city like bees.

"Mobile food is one of the best creations, don't you think? No reservations, the food is good, and they're always in a different location." He bit into his taco, getting a little bit of sauce on his chin.

"You've got a little something," I said, pointing to my own chin to show him where.

"Where? Here?" He pointed to his forehead.

"No, here," I said, pointing to the spot again.

"Oh, here?" This time he pointed to his cheek, and I realized he wasn't being dense; he was messing with me.

"No, here," I said, wiping the spot with my thumb.

"Oh, *there*. I never would have found that spot, thank you." He seemed very pleased with himself.

I went back to my own taco, praying to any god or goddess that would listen that I wouldn't spill anything on myself. Things were in my favor as we both finished without any incident and then walked a few streets down to find an ice cream truck for dessert.

"You have a little something here," Fin said, pointing to his chin. I played along like he had.

"Oh, here? Or how about here?" I pointed to random places on my face until he grabbed my chin and licked the ice cream from my face.

"There." I froze as I looked deep into his eyes. His eyelashes were short, but they were so thick it almost looked like he was wearing mascara.

"Thank you," I whispered as his gaze moved from my eyes to my lips. I licked them reflexively. Just before I realized I had ice cream running down my arm.

"Uh," I said, laughing a little as I realized he had ice cream on his arm, too. Luckily he'd pushed up his sleeves so he didn't ruin his shirt, but still. We both had ice cream all over. I couldn't help staring at him. What was it about a man's forearm that was so seductive?

"Let me get some napkins," he said, handing me the still-melting ice cream to hold. He came back with a huge stack of napkins and proceeded to try to clean my arm and eat his ice cream at the same time.

"Ahhh," he said, squinching his face up. "Brain freeze." I burst out laughing and ended up dropping both cones.

"Aw, I guess that's the end of that," I said. We finished cleaning up, but my arms were still sticky. I hoped Fin didn't notice.

"Well, the ice cream was a bit of a fail. Let's go for bowls next time instead of cones?" Fin said as we strolled down the street.

"Next time?"

"Of course. Didn't we already talk about the third date? The flowers? Ice cream or gelato in a bowl is also part of the third date." He said it as if it was a statement of fact.

"Are these rules written down somewhere? Can I get a copy?"

He stopped me in the street and kissed my chin, just barely avoiding my lips. "I'll work on it for you."

I didn't want the date to end, but end it had to. Carl drove us back to my apartment and stopped the car, but Finn grabbed my arm to stop me from getting out. "You know how at the end of the first date, there's that moment when you say goodbye and you have to decide if you really want the date to end?"

Usually on my first dates, I had to avoid being kissed, or groped, or agreeing to a second date. Just thinking about it reminded me of how many terrible first dates I'd been on. There had been some good ones, my last boyfriend Ben being one of the exceptions. I still missed him, but it had been one of those situations where he loved me more than I loved him, and I stayed with him for longer than I should have. He was off in Texas now working for a tech company.

"Yes, I do."

"Well, I was wondering how you would feel about this date not ending? At least not ending right now. I'd…like to spend some more time with you," he said, stroking the bare skin on my arm and causing my skin to ripple with goosebumps. "But if you want to call it a night, that's also fine." His hand left my skin, and I almost grabbed it to bring it back. No one had touched me like that in a while, and I hadn't known how much I craved it until I got a little taste of it again.

I didn't want to say goodnight. Not yet.

"I'd like to spend some more time with you, Fin." He exhaled and smiled.

"I was hoping you'd say that. I know I said if you wanted to call it a night, you could, but I probably would have spent a lot of time convincing you otherwise." His hand went back to my arm, dancing up to my shoulder and then down to my hand, and then, after a pause, to my thigh. Oh. Was that where we were going?

I must have flinched just a tiny bit because his hand withdrew.

"I'm not asking you to spend the night with me like that, Marisol. We can do whatever you're comfortable with. I'll behave." His eyes sparked. "Or, I'll *try* to behave. But I think I would enjoy you punishing me."

My entire body went hot and then cold and then hot again at his words and their underlying meaning. He knew exactly what he was implying.

Part of me thought that it would be a wise idea to get out of the car and call it a night.

I told that part of myself to shut up.

Should have listened.

To keep some sort of control of the situation, I asked if we could stay at my place. Of course, I said this before I could mentally do a walkthrough and make sure I didn't have anything incriminating or disgusting out in the open.

But Fin seemed to anticipate this and waited a few feet from my door as I unlocked it. "If you need a minute, I can wait," he said, crossing his arms and leaning against the wall.

"Just...don't go anywhere."

"Wouldn't dream of it."

I was rather proud of my apartment, for what it was. Okay, so it was in a sketchy neighborhood and the police were frequently called, and my upstairs neighbor wouldn't stop playing the same three chords on his guitar, but I'd done the best I could with my meager savings and some thrift store finds, and classed it up a bit.

Still, it wasn't what Fin was used to, that much I knew. The wealth disparity between me and my friends had never been much of a big deal. I'd grown up with money, and I knew if I went to my parents on

bended knee and begged them to buy me a pricey apartment and give me an allowance, they'd welcome me back with open arms.

But I didn't want that. I'd escaped from them (just barely) and I liked doing things on my own.

After a quick dash through the place, putting things away and hiding my dirty underwear in the hamper, I made sure any other embarrassing things were tucked out of view.

"Okay, come in," I said, a little breathless from the rushing around.

"Are you sure?" He hovered on the threshold, both hands braced on the doorway. "Are all the monsters shoved away in your closet?" I wasn't sure if that was a metaphor.

"I don't have any monsters, Fin," I said, stepping backwards. I had no idea where that had come from, but I was going to go with it.

"Everyone has monsters, Marisol." His face got serious as he took a step inside.

Yes. Everyone did have monsters.

Fin looked around and smiled. "This is… cozy."

"Cozy is a nice word for small," I said, glaring at him and leaning on the back of the couch.

"No, that's not true. Cozy means…cozy. Comforting. Nice. I like it, I really do."

"Well, it's not much." I was very conscious of the faded rug and the threadbare spots on the couch, and the stack of magazines under one of the chair legs.

"It's something. It's great." We stood there for a moment, both of us awkward.

"Do you want some coffee?"

"That would be nice." I moved to the coffeemaker and filled it up with water.

"How do you take it?"

"Why don't you guess and surprise me?" I gave him a look, but he just kept exploring. "These are really great," he said, pointing to some of the framed photographs above my television.

"Oh, thanks. I took them." I didn't want to brag, but I was pretty proud of how nice a composition they made.

"Really?"

"Are you surprised?" I spooned coffee into the filter. I wished I had fresh ground and a percolator, but that couldn't be helped now. At least the coffee was fresh.

"Not at all," Fin said, leaning close to examine one of the photographs of a child chasing a runaway leaf in the park. Her hair streamed behind her as her hands reached out, trying to grasp the leaf that was just out of reach.

Now I had to decide how Fin wanted his coffee. My first thought was black, but then I reconsidered. Fin was more complicated than that. Maybe I was reading too much into this, but something told me to grab the French vanilla creamer from the fridge.

"If this coffee is wrong, it's your fault for not telling me how you want it," I said as my ancient coffeemaker struggled to work.

He looked back at me and took his coat off, draping it over the couch. "I'm sure it will be fine."

I didn't know about that, but then I filled two cups and added identical amounts of the creamer until the coffee was a nice tan color.

Fin sat on the couch as I brought the cups over. I handed his to him, and he looked at it and then sniffed it. "French vanilla?"

I nodded.

His face split into a grin and he laughed. "That's exactly right."

"Really?" I was still skeptical.

"Really," he said, taking a sip and closing his eyes in relish. "Yup. Perfect." It was crappy cheap coffee, but he was acting as if it was nectar of the gods. He was so sweet.

We sipped our coffee in silence, but it wasn't uncomfortable. It was…cozy. I caught Fin smiling at me over the rim of his mug. I looked down and blushed. "Stop it."

"What? I'm not allowed to admire you?" Admire me? Nobody had ever said that to me before.

"So, here's a question for you. Are you paying attention?" I set my cup down and leaned forward. I knew I was playing with fire, but the flames were too hypnotic.

He put his cup down and leaned toward me.

"I'm paying attention to you. Only you. Your lips," he said, reaching out and brushing them with a feather-light touch. "Your hair. Your eyes." His hand skimmed my hair and then cupped my cheek. "You're a fascinating study, Marisol Everly."

"You too," I said, reaching out and pushing his hair back. It flopped back to the same place as soon as I moved my hand, which made me laugh. My thumb traced his lips. They were lush, for a man's. He parted them slightly and his tongue flicked out and tasted my thumb.

There was a single moment of hesitation. That suspension between standing still and surging forward.

"What about your rules?" he asked, almost making me jump.

"I think I might be able to break a few of them. For you."

He smiled and moved his hand to hold the back of my head. "Then if we're going big, we should go hard, don't you agree?" My muscles tightened with the words "big" and "hard."

It had been a while since I'd had anything that was big or hard, other than my bunny vibrator, and lately it just hadn't been doing the job.

But rules. I had rules. I had….

"Yes. Big and hard," my mouth said just before his lips closed over mine.

Chapter
Four

I knew he was only in town for three weeks. I knew he had a job that caused him to never be in the same place for more than a few weeks. I knew that I knew next to nothing about him, just what I'd learned in the past twenty-four hours and what Rory had told me.

There were so many reasons to tell him to stop when he kissed me, but when those reasons went to battle against the feel of his lips on mine. The heat his touch ignited, and the things he awakened in me that I'd thought were dormant. Or at least they'd been in hibernation for a very, VERY long time.

One of the reasons I had rules was to weed out the guys who were worth it. It was so easy to tell them that I didn't kiss on the first date, then they would "have to run to the office," and would subsequently never call me again. Self-preservation. Or maybe heart preservation.

And then Fin showed up. I'd known that Rory, Sloane, and Chlo were setting me up with him from the first moment that Rory mentioned him, but I'd been willing to go for it, unlike all the other times they'd tried to set me up.

This didn't feel like a set-up. It felt like….

His hand on the back of my head, pulling me close so he could kiss me harder. His lips, firm and demanding, but hesitating before he pushed, letting me come to him first. His other hand on my waist, pulling me so our bodies were almost completely connected.

Rules. What rules?

I separated my lips at the flick of his tongue, letting him in. For two practical strangers, we certainly had kissing chemistry. You never really knew when you started talking with someone if you would have verbal and physical chemistry.

This was more than chemistry.

I heard noises coming from my throat, and we were both gasping in between kisses. The closer we got, the closer we needed to get. I wanted to devour him.

It didn't take long for our hands to start working at removing our irritating clothing. I was working on getting the buttons on his shirt undone, cursing each and every one of them for impeding my access to Fin's skin.

And then there were two hands pushing me away and his mouth separating from mine.

"Marisol, if we don't stop now, there won't be any stopping."

Really? I hadn't figured that out. My hands were still pulling at the buttons on his shirt.

"Marisol." His hands gently removed mine from his shirt. What was he doing? What happened to big and hard?

I finally looked up at his face. His hair was all over the place, his lips were red and swollen, and his eyes were dark and hungry.

"What?" I wanted to kick myself for the way I snapped at him, but I was worked up and he'd put the brakes on. If I stopped and thought about what I was doing, I knew that I would remember all the reasons why this was a bad idea and why I shouldn't continue with it.

"I think we should stop."

And as soon as he said it, I realized he was right. What the hell were we doing?

"Of course," I said, leaning away from him. I was grateful we were on the couch, because I didn't think my legs would have supported me.

"I...I think I should go now," he said, practically leaping from the couch, snatching his jacket, and throwing it on.

"You don't have to leave, Fin."

"No, no. I do. I'll call you later. Bye." And before I knew what was happening, he was slamming the door and I was sitting on my couch with bruised lips and a shattered ego.

"So he just left. Took off," Chloe said, using her hand to mime a taking off motion.

"Pretty much," I said. This time I was the one with my head on the table. "I mean, I thought if anyone was going to freak out, it would be me."

"Maybe you're more alike than you thought. Interesting. But back to the leaving. Everything was going okay, right?"

"Better than okay." It was one of the best first dates I'd ever had. I finally lifted my head and stared into my latte. Bad idea. The barista had made a foam heart. I grabbed a spoon and swirled until the heart was no more.

"Look, why didn't you call Rory or Sloane about this? You know I'm kind of the last person to ask about guys." While this was true, it was also true that Chloe gave good advice. And she didn't have a lot of dating history with men to cloud her judgment.

"But you're my bestie. My homegirl. My boo. I talk to you about everything." That made Chloe smile and give me a bite of her chocolate-filled croissant.

"And you're mine. I have no idea what is wrong with him, but he sounds like an idiot. Maybe he had a problem with his equipment? Maybe he's got a crooked penis." Her eyes widened at the thought.

"I could deal with a crooked penis. It's the leaving without an explanation that I can't deal with. If he had just said, 'Marisol, I'm sorry, but I have a crooked penis and I'm ashamed of it and I need to go,' that wouldn't have been a big deal. It's the not knowing that is driving me crazy."

I'd called and texted Fin, but hadn't heard back. I'd had a mad idea of going to his hotel, but that seemed a little too Crazy Stalker Girl, so I decided to go out to brunch with Chloe instead. And mope.

"It's probably something I did. It usually is." I took a gulp of my latte, burned my tongue, and then choked.

"Whoa there, Tiger. Easy on the latte. As much as I would enjoy giving you mouth to mouth, it might confuse our friendship."

"True," I said, gulping from a glass of ice water.

Chloe started listing more reasons that Fin could have left, some more ridiculous than the crooked penis. I was about to beg her to stop when my phone started going off.

"It's him," I said, staring at my phone, but not moving to actually answer it. After so much silence, it was like something out of a dream to actually hear from him.

"What are you doing, you fool? Answer it!" Chloe picked up the phone and shoved it toward my face, swiping her finger across the screen.

"H-hello?" I said, trying to take the phone from Chloe and put it up to my ear at the same time.

"Hello, Marisol." His voice was crisp and formal. The opposite of how it had been last night. Well, at least before he'd put the brakes on our runaway train of romance.

"Hi, Fin," I said, smacking myself in the face because I'd already greeted him. Chloe was watching me, and I could tell she wished we were alone so I could put him on speakerphone and she could eavesdrop.

"Hi," he said, sounding as dorky as I did.

"I wanted to apologize for last night," he said at the exact same time I said, "I'm sorry things were so weird last night." This caused us both to laugh, which broke the ice just a bit. I nodded to Chloe and got up from the table, walking to a private corner behind a large potted plant so I wouldn't disturb the other customers. Also, so Chloe wouldn't make weird faces at me.

"So, last night," I said.

"Last night was not my finest hour."

"I thought the kissing part was good. Was it not good for you?"

He sighed and was silent for so long I thought the call had dropped.

"Yesterday was amazing. Last night was…yes, the kissing was more than good, I'd say. At least for me. You are very talented, Marisol."

"Well, in addition to my Master's degrees in Business Admin and Education, I also have a Master's in Kissology." He let out a burst of unexpected laughter.

"Those must have been very…informative classes."

"Oh, they were and the coursework was exhausting."

"I can only imagine." The tone of his voice was reminding me of our "coursework" from last night.

"We need to talk about…what happened after the kissing. When you jumped up from the couch as if you were on fire and left without

an explanation. Now, if I were to listen to my mother's advice, it would be to shut up and pretend it never happened. But, unfortunately for you, I've spent most of my life trying to not be my mother. So. What happened after the kissing?"

My speech seemed to stun him momentarily.

"What happened after the kissing. Well. That is a loaded question that would require quite an explanation."

"Wow, you're long-winded with your explanations." I just wanted him to get to the point and tell me about his crooked penis so I could assure him that I didn't care a whit about it and we could move on to date three.

"I…I really don't think this is the kind of thing I can do over the phone. Can we meet?" Well, I wasn't looking my best at the moment.

"Sure. How about my apartment? An hour?"

"See you then."

He hung up without any further pleasantries and I went back to Chloe, who was bouncing in her seat for information.

"Well?"

I sat down slowly, picking up my half-finished latte and sipping it carefully.

"Mari." She knew I was teasing her, but I wanted to let her suffer for a few seconds. It was good for her. Taught her patience.

"You whore, tell me."

"Well, it was kind of awkward and he didn't really give me an explanation, but we're going to meet up at my apartment and talk. So I'm guessing it's more than just a crooked penis."

And now I was freaking out. If his issue needed an explanation that had to be delivered in person, it was probably…delicate. Or explosive. Maybe he had an explosive penis.

"That doesn't sound good. That probably means he's a serial killer. I should hide in your bedroom, just to make sure." For Chloe, this was a perfectly reasonable thing to do.

"Chlo. Would Rory let me go out with a serial killer?"

"Only if she didn't know he was a serial killer."

This was getting us nowhere.

"I know if I don't let you come, then you're going to barge in, aren't you?"

"I might."

I sighed. "Well, we need to get going, because he's coming over in an hour and I need to make myself presentable."

"You look fine. If he can't appreciate you as you are, then he doesn't deserve you." Typical best friend, thinking the world shined out of my ass, and any guy who didn't think I was perfect wasn't worth my time.

"I've known the man for all of two days. I'd like to give the allure that I look fantastic all the time. At least for a week."

I paid the bill and we headed back to my place.

Chapter Five

"Nope," Chloe said as I tried on yet another dress.

"God, what do you want from me? You've turned down every single one so far. I don't have a whole lot of clothes, you know." My few designer pieces had been found after much thrift shop searching and were very dear to me.

"I want you to be yourself. Right now you look like you're trying too hard," she said from her position on my bed, a pillow under her chin.

"Well, if you're such a fashion genius, what should I wear?" I pulled my dress over my head and put my hands on my hips.

"This," she said, holding up a dark blue top I didn't even know that I owned, and a flared black skirt. "And some black boots. Trust me."

I was skeptical, but I put the outfit on. I had to admit that it was really cute.

"Whoa, too much swirling there, babe. You're gonna need to wear some tights or something so you don't show him EVERYTHING on the second date."

"Technically this is the third date," I said, pulling some tights that I'd worn all of once out of my drawer. I hated the damn things, but Chloe was right. I couldn't flounce around showing everyone my lady business.

I left my hair down because it was behaving today, but I gave it a good brush before I applied some makeup and posed for Chloe to show the final effect.

"I'd do you," was her response to the outfit. "Also, you might want to stop fiddling with the hem of that skirt or else he'll know you're nervous."

I didn't know I'd been doing that, but as soon as Chloe pointed it out, I was conscious of it. "Thanks. Now I'm even more paranoid than I already was."

She got up and stood behind me in the mirror, putting her chin on my shoulder. "Don't be paranoid. You're beautiful and smart and funny, and he'd be a dumbass not to see that. So there." She smacked me on the butt and I winced. "Now go get him."

I'd managed to get Chloe to go back to her apartment by agreeing to go clubbing with her at a gay bar. Five minutes before he was supposed to pick me up, Fin was at my door in a lovely gray shirt, black pants, and a light purple tie.

"Wow," I said because I couldn't help myself. He had one hand behind his back and revealed a bouquet of lilacs. As soon as the smell hit me, I grinned like an idiot and had to resist the urge to throw my arms around his neck. Lilacs weren't a very easy flower to find, but somehow he had.

"Wow doesn't do you justice," he said, handing me the flowers. I closed my eyes and inhaled deeply, memories flooding my mind. I hoped tonight I could make new ones.

"Once again, I'm so sorry about bolting last night. It was nothing you did, and I know that sounds like a line, but it's the truth. I know we just met, but I really like you and I'd like to spend more time with you." I stepped aside to let him into the apartment, which was a hell of a lot cleaner than it had been last night. Actually, it was probably cleaner than it had ever been.

"I wish you could have told me this last night instead of just leaving. That was kind of a dick move, you know." He chuckled as he followed me toward the kitchen. I had to find a glass bottle to put the flowers in, since I didn't actually own a vase. In fact, I couldn't remember the last time I'd needed one.

"Yeah, it was. But running seems so much more easy than actually telling the truth." He still hadn't really told me anything, other than he liked me.

"So what is the truth?" I asked, filling up the bottle and sticking the flowers in it before setting it on the middle of my kitchen counter. "Chloe thinks you have a crooked penis, and I said that I wouldn't care. I'd get over it. I mean, by the time we got to that stage. We were pretty close last night."

"Yes," he said, "we were." Then he seemed to absorb the rest of what I'd said. "Wait, you thought I had a crooked penis?"

I shrugged one shoulder. "It was a possibility. Is that it? Crooked penis?"

He laughed, throwing his head back. "No. There is nothing wrong with my penis. I've had plenty of compliments on it." I was sure he had, along with compliments on the rest of him. From what I'd seen so far, it was all complimentary.

"Look," he said, stepping closer to me. "I think we moved a little too fast last night. Maybe we should...put on the brakes a little and go slow. See where this leads." He was asking me to let what happened last night go and pretend it didn't happen.

I guessed I could do that.

"Deal. But don't let it happen again," I said, admonishing him with my finger.

"Deal." He lunged out and bit the tip of my finger.

This time Fin took me to a performance of the play *Noises Off*, which I'd seen before, but not in a long time.

"I wasn't sure if you liked musicals or not, so I figured this was a safe choice," he said as he bought the tickets.

"When it comes to musicals, as long as it's not *Cats!*, I'm good."

He shuddered at the mention of *Cats!*. "Agreed. *Cats!* is pretty much the worst thing ever to happen to musical theater." A straight guy who could admit he loved musicals. Where the hell had he come from and how was I on a date with him?

After we laughed our faces off at the play, we went to dinner at a little hole-in-the-wall Thai place that Fin said he'd seen good reviews about.

"Have you been to Thailand?" I asked after we ordered.

He nodded. "A few times. It's one of the most beautiful places in the world, but, like I said, I didn't get to see much of it. I'd be in the middle of these meetings and I'd look out the window and imagine just getting up, leaving the room and going to the beach."

"And what stopped you?"

He smiled. "My father's wrath. Losing my job. It's true that I don't love it like I used to, but that doesn't mean I want to quit. Besides, it's kind of impossible to get out of a family business, as you probably know from Rory." The only difference was that Rory adored her job and she'd worked her entire life with the one goal of working with her father. It was rare, I supposed, to actually choose the same thing your parents wanted for you. I certainly hadn't.

"But I don't want to sound like I'm whining. I have opportunities some people would give anything for and I don't want to seem ungrateful. What about your family? I've been going on about myself. I want to know about you." Right. Me. I'd much rather talk about him.

"There's not much to tell. I told you about my grandmother and that's…that's really all there is to know." I didn't want to get into my family history this early in a relationship. Most guys were satisfied with me saying that I didn't want to talk about it, but I didn't think Fin would be that easy to distract.

He wasn't.

"It's okay if you don't want to talk about it. We all have our secrets." From the way he said it, I could tell that there was a lot more to him leaving last night than I could probably imagine. Much more than a crooked penis.

"Thanks. I really appreciate that." Our food came and we talked about work and school.

"So, are you one of those people who just never leaves school and gets a million degrees?" Fin asked, swiping a shrimp from my plate and flashing me a smile that said he knew he was going to get away with it. If only he wasn't so good looking. I would have a much easier time resisting him if he was a little less attractive. But it just wasn't how he was put together. It was the way his eyes flashed, letting me know that he had devilish thoughts in his mind, and the way his smile tipped just slightly to the side.

"No. I just want to defer my loans as long as possible." I had added up how much I owed, and the figure made me want to curl up in the fetal position and cry.

"That makes sense," he said, nodding.

I sighed. "I don't know. I guess I just want to prove that I'm smart." It sounded so stupid when I said it out loud like that, and I cringed inwardly and wished I could take it back.

"Who would say you weren't smart? I knew you were smart five seconds after meeting you." That was very flattering. I couldn't remember exactly what I'd said to give him that impression. It must have been something good. Maybe Chloe could fill me in on my supposed brilliance.

I shook my head and tried to put it into words. I'd been asked this question over and over and I didn't have a set answer. "Listen, I'm not going to go into my family situation. I mean, I don't normally go into it with people I've just met. It tends to change how people see me and I don't like that. Let's just say I'm being totally mature and trying to prove to my parents and the rest of my relatives that I can make it on my own, and that I don't need them."

Fin thought about that for a minute. I could see him rolling it over in his mind. Yes, I'd told him that I didn't discuss this kind of thing with new people, but somehow I knew Fin would understand in the way Rory understood my family drama. We might have completely different lives, but families were all pretty much the same when you got down to it.

Complicated.

"I get it. I do. Plus, you get to be called doctor and you don't have to go to medical school. Unless you wanted to, of course." I'd toyed with the idea of medical school once upon a time. The reason I'd rejected it was because my parents had been semi-supportive of the idea. Well, as long as I went into something prestigious. Like

neuroscience or cardiology. I could have gone into pediatrics and stuck it to them, but instead I went into something that would piss them off even more. Education.

Just the memory of the look on my mother's face when I'd told her made me smile to this day. It was second only to telling her that my childhood boyfriend and I had broken up, and weren't getting married after all. Ironic, considering Rory's mother wanted her to marry Fin and here I was on a date with him.

My mother would be all over Fin like a new exclusive pair of Manolos. Even more so. He was exactly what she'd wanted for her little girl. So much for disappointing my parents. But I was going to keep Fin a secret from them as long as humanly possible. Forever, if I could, depending on how this went. I was getting a little ahead of myself.

"Let's talk about something else. Tell me something...tell me something about your grandmother. Your face lights up when you talk about her." Not on purpose.

I remembered the lilacs that were waiting for me back at the apartment. I almost couldn't wait to get back to them to bury my face in their blooms and lose myself in their scent.

"Well, her name was Rosemary and she was terrifying, at least to a lot of people. Very strict, very old-fashioned. No elbows on the table, tea in the sunroom, no yelling, crossed ankles, the whole shebang. She tried teaching me to be a lady, but I don't think much of it stuck, although I definitely hear her voice in my head whenever I put my elbows on the table, or use the wrong spoon like a caveman. The horror!" I used to mess with her and do things like that on purpose. Instead of getting mad, she would just laugh and tell me that I was her wild child.

Of course my mother would pick up the slack and give me a good tongue-lashing later, but Gram never yelled at me once for breaking one of her precious rules. As a result, I actually tried, because I wanted to make her happy. To this day I could probably balance a book on my head, cross a room, and sit in a chair without having it fall to the floor. When you learn something like that in your childhood, it doesn't really go away.

"What did she look like?" Fin seemed actually interested, so I continued.

"Well, she was tall and she had the most glorious hair. It was long and thick and curly, and she took great pride in it. She used to let me brush it and braid it. I always wished mine was the same shade of silver." She would always hum when I brushed her hair and I found myself humming one of her songs right in front of Fin.

He smiled and I blushed.

"Okay, that's enough of that," I said, and went back to eating. He just laughed at me and stole another shrimp.

"You are cruising for a bruising."

I meant it as a joke, but there was an odd look that passed over his face when I said it. It was gone so quickly, like a blink, that I wasn't sure if I'd even seen it in the first place. Could have been a trick of the light.

"So, would you like to get dessert?" he said.

"What kind of a question is that? Who says no to dessert?"

He shook his head. "I have no idea. No one I'd be friends with."

He paid the bill again, and I was starting to feel a little odd about making him pay for so many meals, even though that was traditional dating practice.

"So, you get to pick where we go since you know the city better than I do." It was a balmy evening, the heat wafting up from the pavement.

"How do you feel about gelato?" I asked as we strolled down the street.

"I'm definitely in favor of it. Plus we did agree that ice cream was part of the third date."

I took him to one of those tiny places that's crammed in between two buildings and only has one table, which was almost always occupied. I got sea salt caramel and Fin went for dark chocolate cherry. We swapped bites with each other as we walked down the street. Pedestrians streamed around us, each on their own mission.

"Tomorrow is Monday," I said, realizing too late that I had to go to class tomorrow. Hell and damnation. Why had I decided to complete my degree early by taking summer classes? It had seemed smart at the time, but now I was cursing myself.

"Yes, yes it is. I'm guessing you have a full schedule." He tossed the empty gelato container in a trashcan.

"I have class nearly all day, and I have a study session and I also have a meeting. God, I'd nearly forgotten. You distracted me. I wasn't paying attention." I bumped him with my shoulder.

"I hope it was a good distraction."

"Very." He pulled me to a stop and turned to face me. I knew that he was going to kiss me, and I raised myself on my tiptoes in preparation. He leaned down and brought his face toward mine and…

Pulled away at the last second.

I slammed back down on my heels and nearly lost my balance.

"Is something wrong?"

He looked away from me. "No. Nothing. I just think that you have a busy day tomorrow, and I have a busy day, and we should…probably call it a night." It was like being dunked in a bucket of ice. Things were so easy and free with Fin, and then it was as if he slammed a door in my face, turning into a stranger that was cold and distant and locked in his own head.

"Absolutely. You're right. At least one of us should be responsible." My voice was false in my own ears and made me cringe.

He started walking again, and I had to rush to keep up with his long legs. I took two steps for every one of his. We'd walked to the theater on this date, since it wasn't that far from my apartment. I wondered if Carl got the night off, or if he still had to be at the ready to drive Fin around. My mother had a driver, and the poor man was on call twenty-four hours a day, but she paid him very well, so I guessed it worked out.

"Is everything okay? You're acting like you did last night when you left, and we made a deal that you wouldn't do that again." I grabbed his hand to make him stop and face me. It was exhausting keeping up with him.

He stopped and I nearly crashed into him. "I know I've been acting strangely, and I'm sorry again. Maybe this isn't the best idea. I knew you were a bad idea the second I saw you at the bar, but I'm a sucker for educated women who aren't afraid to say what they think. Plus, you already had the Rory Clarke Seal of Approval, so that was another bonus."

"So what's the problem? Do you have some deep dark secret that you're afraid to share with me because you think it's going to make me run the other way?" It didn't take a Master's degree to figure it out. At first glance, he seemed to have his shit together, but on further inspection, there was something dark hovering beneath the surface. He just hid it well.

"This isn't a joke, Marisol. There are things that I could tell you that…"

"That what?" Apart from the fact that I didn't like him behaving so bizarrely, I was also exceedingly curious about this secret. What could be so bad? The possibilities were endless—far beyond that of a crooked penis.

"That what, Fintan?" I hadn't used his full first name before, but this seemed like as good a time as any.

He leaned in close and a slow smile spread across his face that sent a shiver down my spine. "Things that would make your skin crawl."

Chapter Six

For a moment, I didn't breathe as Fin's eyes flicked across my face, testing my reaction.

"I'm not scared," I said, sounding like a little girl who had just been dared to steal a pair of earrings from a store in the mall. His face moved just a breath closer. Close enough that I could count his eyelashes and smell the chocolate from the gelato on his breath.

My entire body was screaming for him to kiss me, to touch me, to do SOMETHING to me. I'd never ached for someone more. I didn't know I could feel this way, as if something was throbbing and growing inside me, and if I didn't let it out, or satisfy it, it would consume me.

It was like being on fire.

"I'm not scared of you, Fin," I said, my voice so quiet I didn't even know if I'd spoken aloud.

"You should be, sweet Marisol." His voice caressed my name, played with it, made me think about bare skin sliding against sheets, and moans of pleasure and all manner of fantasies I'd never entertained with another person.

"You're so, *so* sweet." He snapped his eyes closed and stepped away from me. He might as well have shoved me to the ground. "I'm going to get a cab and go back to my place. I don't think we should see each other anymore. At least not alone. Tell Rory nice try, but we're not…suited for one another. Goodbye." At least he looked at me when he said it. He had the decency to do that.

He also had the decency to hail me a cab and hand the driver a fifty to take me home, even though it was only a short walk. As the cab pulled away, I watched him standing there, silhouetted by the lights from buildings and vehicles.

I imagined screaming at the cabbie to stop, getting out and rushing toward him, throwing my arms around his neck and kissing him passionately. But as he vanished from my view, the idea of doing that got further away, and soon I turned around and stared straight ahead.

I had the cabbie take me right to Chloe's place. I definitely didn't want to be alone right now, and those damned lilacs were still at my apartment. I texted her before I got there, to make sure she wasn't indisposed with someone before I barged in. It had happened a few times in the past.

"Aw, babe." She greeted me with open arms. "Men are dicks."

"I don't think he's a dick, honestly. Despite the fact that he definitely was hot one minute and cold the next and promised me he wouldn't do it anymore, and then did it anyway." Fin wasn't trying to hurt me. He wasn't trying to be an asshole. It felt like he was, but the way he'd looked at me….

No one had ever looked at me that way before. Ever.

Chloe was skeptical, but she played the best friend role and comforted me with her shoulder and food, wine, and bad television.

"Do you mind if I stay over?" I asked as I finished my second glass of wine. So what if I had classes tomorrow, and one of my event planning meetings? I needed this tonight.

"What's mine is yours, girlfriend." I'd thought about moving in with Chloe before, but we both really liked our own space. She was my best friend in the entire world, but I didn't know if we could actually live with each other without it ruining the friendship. It was a risk neither of us was willing to take for the sake of lower rent.

"Are you sure you're okay?" She handed me a cup of tea after I'd finished the wine and she'd made a bed up for me on the couch. I had several sets of clothes here, but I'd have to go home and pick up my homework and notes before class.

"Yeah. I'll get over it. Good thing it ended now and not further in where feelings had actually been involved." I tried to laugh, but it was false. My feelings had been involved. Despite only knowing the man for a few days, I'd started caring for him. Not falling. Not love. Not yet. Like. I was definitely in like with him. Deep like.

And now it was over. Ended just as soon as it had begun. I hoped Rory wouldn't be mad at me and it wouldn't make things uncomfortable with her parents. They were still harboring the delusion that Rory and Fin were somehow destined to be together, and if they only wished and pushed them together hard enough, it would happen.

"Don't tell Rory yet, okay? I really don't want her to feel bad for setting us up and it falling apart. Give it a few days to simmer down. I hope he doesn't say anything to her." Maybe I should just send him a message and ask him not to, but that would mean contacting him, and my ego was still bruised.

Decisions, decisions.

"Boys are awful," I said. She patted my head sympathetically and we sat together for a while, not saying a word. Finally I told Chlo I was tired and wanted to get some sleep.

"Goodniiiiiight, sweeeeeeetheart," Chloe sang as she headed to bed after giving me a huge hug. She had work the next morning, so I didn't even need to set an alarm to make sure I got up.

As I closed my eyes and tried to fall asleep, all I saw were Fin's eyes, and that smile. And the words. *Things that would make your skin crawl.*

What things? What kind of things could he possibly think would make me feel that way? There were a myriad of possibilities.

I spent most of the night going through them, and by the time Chloe came to wake me up, I was no closer to figuring it out. Maybe if I knew him better, but I didn't. Hell, I hadn't even known him for a week.

Fintan Herald was a mystery. A sexy mystery wrapped in a dark riddle. Delicious as chocolate and just as addicting, and very bad for my health.

Midway through my Social Contexts of Education class, I made the decision. I texted Fin and asked him not to tell Rory that her plan to set us up had imploded. Well, I didn't put it exactly like that in the text. I tried to be more…discreet.

As I headed to get some coffee before my next class, I nearly crashed into someone who wasn't watching where they were going.

"Oh, I'm sorry," I started to say, but then I looked up and saw exactly who I'd crashed into.

"Are you stalking me? Is that your dirty little secret?" Why did that sound so sexy when I said it out loud? There was definitely something to mysterious guys being more attractive than guys who put it all out there.

"I wasn't stalking you. Um, gently following would be the better term." For the first time since I'd met him, he seemed unsure. Nervous.

"So remember last night when I said all those things and then put you in a cab and sent you away? Could you maybe…forget that happened?" I almost laughed at how sweet he sounded. There was a little bit of awkward hidden under the polished clothing and perfect smile.

"I don't know. Give me a reason to." He pulled me aside, up against the corner of the building. My skin tingled with anticipation, and I could feel that ache racing through my body just like it had last night.

I was no virgin, and I'd had my share of pleasurable sexual experiences. But I'd never wanted anyone the way I wanted Fin. Like I'd die if I couldn't have him, which was ridiculous. No one ever died from lack of sex. That I knew of.

"You've completely wrecked me, Marisol. Destroyed me from the second I met you. I can't stop thinking about you. You've made work very difficult, I'll have you know." Like it was my fault because I was *so* sexy and *so* seductive. The thought was almost ludicrous. I'd be laughing if I could actually breathe.

He was dismantling me with his words. *No one* had ever said such things to me. I didn't know men outside of movies and/or romance novels that said such things, and not to girls like me. Not to girls like me that they'd just met.

"I'd like to try this with you. If you want. We can take things slow. As slow as you want, and we'll cross any bridges we need to cross when

we need to cross them. I'm not making much sense, am I?" He reached up and touched my face so lightly, but I held his hand there so he wouldn't take it away, wouldn't pull back from me.

His body pressed up against mine, pushing me into the cool brick of the building. The uneven surface scraped against my back. I wondered what it would be like if we did more up against this brick wall. Would it leave a mark?

"Well, I could blame you for the fact that I learned next to nothing in the class I just attended, and I didn't get any sleep last night either. What do you have to say to that?"

A smile flitted across his mouth. "I say…want to get some coffee?"

"And I say, don't you have somewhere else to be?" He shook his head slowly and stepped away from me, but offered me his hand. "I don't want to be anywhere but here with you."

I knew I was letting him get away with being sweet to me now to make up for being not so sweet last night. For the second time. But I took his hand as we walked down the street to the Starbucks, hoping that this time he wouldn't run away. This time he would keep being sweet.

Chapter
Seven

Coffee was perfect, but it ended too quickly.

"When can I see you again?" he asked. I wanted to tell him that I was free that night, but it was probably a good idea to let things cool for a day or two, see if I could wrap my head around everything that had happened. Get my hormones under control, if that was even possible.

"I'll let you know." It was one of those old tricks. Always leave them wanting more. I'd never played those kinds of games before. I'd never been in a situation where I had the chance to. But something told me that Fin liked to play games. Back and forth. Yes and no. I'd always avoided guys like him in the past. Too complicated.

"You don't have to play hard to get. You're already unattainable," he said as we finished our coffees.

"I'm here with you, aren't I? How am I unattainable?" That was crazy talk. He was the one who lived on a different planet.

"I said you were sweet, and I meant it. You're sweet and lovely and much too good for someone like me." There he went again. Mr. Dark and Twisty. "I'm going to ruin you, you know."

Ruin me?

I gave him a look as he walked me back toward the building where my next class was.

"Maybe I want to be ruined a little." If he was doing the ruining.

He shook his head slowly. "I'll see you later."

"See you later." I definitely would. He didn't scare me.

That much.

Sloane called me as I was rushing to my meeting for the Animal Rescue League of Boston. We were organizing a large Adopt-a-Pet Day and I was in charge of finding a venue.

"Hey, Sloane. I can't talk, I'm late, but what's up?" She wouldn't have called if it wasn't important. She would have just texted me.

"Hey, chica. I'm just calling because I'm a little worried about Rory. I think there's something weird going on with her and Lucas, and I thought maybe we should talk to her about it. Or just be there, or whatever. You know. Do the friend thing." I waited for the little electronic man on the crosswalk sign to tell me that I wasn't going to be flattened by a cab before crossing to the other side of the street. I was seriously late at this point.

"Okay, what did you have in mind?"

"I don't know. Maybe I'm just being crazy. Things are nuts at work and I've had too much coffee, and I've started doing that thing where I create problems just so I can solve them, you know?" I was more than familiar with this version of Sloane. Unlike most people, who maybe just got a little hyper on caffeine, Sloane was like a kid high on sugar. And crack. It worked for her since she was in a creative industry, but she might want to tone it down a bit. I told her as much.

"Okay, fine. No big deal. But I have another set for you to try on. I'm messengering it over to your apartment. You'd better have a date in the next week, hopefully with a lovely young man named Fin?"

"Look, hun, I don't have time to get to that right now, but I will call you later. Promise." I hung up and dashed to the elevator before she could say anything else.

Everyone stared at me as I rushed into the room, trying to pull my folder of potential locations out of my bag and sit in my seat at the same time. "Sorry I'm late," I gasped, finally releasing my folder from my purse's clutches. I got a few glares, but for the most part everyone got back on track as Barbara, the head of our group, called our meeting to order.

Once again, I tried to focus on the task at hand, but all I could think of was how itchy my fingers were to text Fin and tell him I was free tonight so I could rush home and put on the lingerie Sloane had sent me. Even if he wasn't going to see it, since we were taking things slow. There was something wonderful about wearing beautiful underwear.

I was able to get my head out of FinLand for enough time to do my little presentation, after which there was a lot of haggling and going back and forth about locations. Inside was nearly impossible with the amount of animals we had, so outside seemed logical to me, but that would require renting a tent, or finding someone who would donate one, which was always tricky.

We voted and the meeting adjourned. It was now up to me to find a tent company who would give us a discounted rate, or donate for the good of puppies and kittens, and report back next week. Fortunately,

I already had a good rapport with several companies. Occupational hazard of doing a lot of charity work.

My stomach screamed at me, begging for food. I realized I hadn't had anything since lunch. I wished I were one of those girls who could not eat for hours and subsist on air, but I definitely wasn't.

I texted Chloe, but she was stuck at work, and Sloane was busy. I didn't really want to see Rory because she was bound to ask questions about Fin, and I didn't really want to deal with that yet.

I had two options. Dine alone or break that little promise I'd made to myself mere hours ago to play hard to get. To give us some space. I didn't want to be one of those girls who just caved for a man. No way. I'd dined alone thousands of times and I could do it again. Yes I could.

To prove that I could do it, I took a cab home and went straight to my fridge to cook myself some dinner. Dinner for one. Just me. No one else.

I still had the lilacs on my counter. They'd had significance for me before I met Fin, and they would after whatever this was ended. Lilacs were mine. I shouldn't have told him those were my favorite flowers. Ah, well. Couldn't do anything about it now.

I put together a quick chicken Caesar salad with some chopped fruit and a glass of wine.

I turned on the television and found a marathon of *Parks and Recreation*. Perfect. Leslie Knope was a strong, independent woman for me to emulate. She'd stand her ground against a sexy man.

I inhaled my salad and finished my wine, and decided it was a dessert night, so I pulled out a mini cheesecake from the freezer and let it thaw.

While I was waiting, I pulled out my phone and started spinning it on the counter. I wasn't normally this bad about being by myself.

My phone buzzed with a new message, dancing away from my hands. I picked it up and saw that it was a message from Fin.

Could you give me a ballpark of when I can see you again?

I bit my lip to stop myself from smiling. I shouldn't be smiling. I should be mad at him for contacting me when I said I would let him know. Mad. I should be mad.

You really are going for stalker status.

There. Let him make something of that.

I can't help it if I want to see you.

Yes, he could. He could very well help it. Who was in charge here?

What happened to taking it slow? ME telling YOU when we we'd see each other again?

There was a long pause and I chewed on my thumbnail as I waited.

I'm impatient.

I rolled my eyes and decided to just call him.

"You know, you're not doing anything to help build your case for getting to see me again," I said by way of a greeting.

"Says who? I'm talking to you, aren't I? You responded to my texts, didn't you?" I almost wished he was here so I could smack the smirk I knew was on his face right off it.

"That doesn't mean I'm not going to change my number and never call you again."

"I know where you live."

"I'll move." I was totally bluffing and we both knew that, but at least he was enough of a gentleman to not point it out.

"Can I see you tomorrow?"

"I have class. And I have to work." I worked a few hours a week selling candles and other scented items at parties. It was fun and I made enough money at it (supplemented by my student loans) to get by. I wished I could work more at a regular job, but even finding something part time that I could work around school was nearly impossible. I'd thought about bartending, but wasn't sure if I wanted to deal with that on top of everything else.

"So? There are plenty of hours in the day where I'm sure you're free. I can meet you."

"Don't *you* have a job?" I was beginning to wonder if Fin's job was just imaginary or if it was just easy, because he seemed to be able to leave whenever he wanted to come stalk me.

"So?"

I sighed in frustration. "I think I can squeeze you in tomorrow. I'll text you for sure. Goodnight."

"Goodnight, Marisol. Until tomorrow." I hung up and stared at my phone. What had just happened?

I shook my head at myself and went to get my now-defrosted cheesecake. I told myself I was only going to eat half, but I ended up eating the whole thing, cursing Fin the entire time.

I needed more willpower. I shouldn't have picked up the phone to call him. His voice did things to my insides and broke down any resistance I might have had.

He was being pushy, and I would have told anyone else in my position to tell him to back the hell off. But I was me and I didn't want to tell him to back off. I wanted to see him just as much as he wanted to see me. It wasn't a crime to want to hang out with someone.

Things that would make your skin crawl.

The words ran through my head over and over as I snuggled into bed that night. I was a fitful sleeper, so one essential was a king-sized bed. It barely fit in my bedroom, but somehow the movers had wedged it in. It was more than enough bed for two people, but no one else had ever slept in it with me. Even when I'd had boyfriends, I'd always stayed at their place. I hadn't wanted to "show them mine" when they'd asked to come to my apartment. Fin was actually the first one.

Fin. I rolled over onto my stomach and buried my face in one of my pillows. I was all twisted up inside, and I didn't know what to do about it.

This wasn't one of those things I could go to my friends about. I had to put on my big girl panties and figure this one out on my own.

Chapter Eight

I slept poorly for the second night in a row and woke up at a level of grumpy that not even two cups of coffee could fix. I was late getting out of the shower, which made me late for class, which made my professor grumpy, since it was a small class and I'd interrupted his lecture with my entrance.

Then I spilled my third cup of coffee in my purse and it was all downhill from there.

I'd said I was going to text Fin, but I didn't really want him to see me like this. My hair was a mess thanks to my short time getting ready, my purse smelled like coffee, and there were splatters all over my skirt.

I was a trainwreck.

Today's not good for me. Raincheck?

I hoped he wouldn't be pissed.

Are you okay? Do you need anything?

His response surprised me. What I really needed was a do-over, and unless he knew some form of time travel, then he was out of luck.

No, but thank you. Until tomorrow?

I crossed my fingers as I wanted for his response. *Until tomorrow.*

The day just got worse, and by the time I was heading home (an hour later than I intended due to an unexpected trip to the library, and the fact that a woman at the candle party couldn't decide between Ocean Breeze and Mango Mambo candles), I was so done with Tuesday.

My phone rang and I checked to see who it was before I answered.

"Hey, Chloe. I've had the most terrible, awful day. Please tell me you're out of work so you can un-suck this day." I heard subway noise in the background.

"As a matter of fact, I'm on my way to your place. I, too, have had a shitty day and I need my BFF. See you in ten minutes?"

"Absolutely."

I dashed home, tore off my coffee-stained clothes, and put on a pair of yoga pants and a baggy t-shirt. It was my loungewear. I pulled my hair off my neck and into a messy bun, and wiped off my makeup.

Much better.

There was a knock at the door and I bounced to answer it.

"I hope you brought something—" I started to say, but it wasn't Chloe on the other side of the door.

It was Fin.

"You're not Chloe," I said, stating the obvious.

"I could if you wanted me to be," he said, his hands in his pockets. He'd obviously just come from the office, complete with crisp purple white-collared shirt, slate gray tie, and black jacket. There was

something so seductive about a man in a suit. It was almost better than a man being naked. I said *almost*.

I sputtered and tried to think of something to say, but then I realized what I was wearing. The absolute *last* thing you would want the guy you'd just met and were interested in to see you dressed in. This was Frump Wear at its finest.

"What are you doing here?" I crossed my arms over my chest to distract him from my bralessness.

"I wanted to see you, and bring you this." He pulled something out of his pocket with a flourish.

It was a rubber duck. An actual rubber duck. Only this rubber duck had little purple flowers all over it that kind of looked like lilacs. As far as presents went, it was sweet and cute and reminiscent of our first date.

It was perfect.

He held the duck out on his palm with a boyish smile and my heart started fluttering. How was it that this guy, this guy who gave me a rubber duck, could be the same guy who said he'd done things that would make me sick? Maybe he had an evil twin.

"It's a stupid gift. I'm sorry," he said, trying to cram the duck back in his pocket, but I snatched it before he could.

"No, it's not a stupid gift." I was about to say something else, but I was interrupted by the arrival of Chloe.

"Well, hello. Am I interrupting something? Do I need to interrupt something?" She held up a bottle of wine, and I congratulated myself on my choice of best friend.

"No, you're not interrupting anything. I was just…dropping by," Fin said, taking a step backwards as if he was about to bolt.

"Don't leave on my account. If you two need to work something out, then I can make myself scarce. I'm not alone. I have my ten-dollar bottle of wine to keep me company. Carry on." She winked at me and also started to back away.

Were both of them going to leave me?

"No, don't go." They both stopped and then looked at each other. Now it was up to me. Great. I could bail on my best friend or I could bail on the adorable guy who'd given me a rubber ducky.

"Look, I see how this is going. Dicks before chicks. I knew this day would come with you, and I'm okay with it. Really. I can call Sloane. Have a good time." Chloe backed away even more, and I didn't know what to say.

"No, no. I wouldn't dream of usurping a BFF," Fin said, shaking his head. I wondered if he really thought that or if he was trying to impress Chloe.

She stared at him for a while. "Nicely done. I hope you're being legit and you're not just saying that because you're trying to butter me up." I almost snorted at the symbiosis of our thinking.

Fin pretended to be scandalized. "I would never lie to the best friend of the woman I'm courting." Courting. It sounded so old-fashioned and delightful at the same time. Any moment he was going to ask if we could go steady.

Chloe scoffed, but held up the bottle of wine.

"We could have a threesome." I wished I could give her a kick in the leg, but she was too far away.

"The more the merrier," Fin said, and they both pushed past me and entered my apartment.

Okay. So we were having a threesome.

"So," Chloe said, pouring Fin a glass of wine as he shucked off his jacket and leaned against the counter like he had nowhere else to be. "What are your intentions with my friend?" She pushed the glass toward him and he took it gingerly, as if it was about to explode.

I sipped at my own glass, wondering why this was happening right at this moment after the crappy day I had. Was I being punished?

"My intentions are entirely honorable," he said, sounding like he was quoting Jane Austen. For all I knew, he was.

"Bullshit," Chloe said, jabbing her finger at him. "I may be a lesbian, but I know more about how men tick than you'd think."

"I wouldn't doubt it for a second," he said.

I had to put a stop to this.

"Okay, pissing contest over. I'm standing right here, and neither one of you owns me. I refuse to be fought over." They both sort of blinked at me as if I'd just announced I was renouncing my worldly possessions and moving to a convent.

"So no more of that. You'll have to learn how to share. Sharing is caring." I sipped my wine and went to sit on the couch. I grabbed a blanket and put it over myself, using it to hide my yoga pants and nippleage.

It only took a few moments for the other two to come join me. I saw a little battle when it came to who got to sit next to me on the couch, and who got the chair. Fin gestured to the couch, stepping back to let Chloe sit with me.

I just rolled my eyes. Honestly.

Chloe didn't stay long, but it was enough time to make the entire room thick with tension and weirdness.

It had been so much easier at the bar, where there were more people and poor lighting, and I'd also had a few more drinks in me. Plus, my outfit had been much cuter.

"Welp, I think I should be heading out," Chloe said, stretching and taking her empty wineglass to the sink.

"Don't leave because of me," Fin said.

"Look, can we all agree that this is an awkward situation and just pretend it never happened? Please?" I asked, getting up to do…something.

"Sure. I'll call you tomorrow, babe," Chloe said, holding her arms out for a hug. "Call me if you need *anything*," she whispered in my ear.

"Why would I need anything? Are you afraid to leave me alone with him?" She was acting strange, and I needed to get to the bottom of it.

"Excuse us," I said before I dragged her to my bedroom and shut the door. "What's going on? Other than the weirdness that just happened in my living room." I made her sit down on my bed. "Is there something wrong with him?"

She shook her head immediately. "No, there's nothing wrong with him other than the fact that he likes you and I'm jealous. There, I said it. I'm a terrible jealous person."

That was unexpected.

"Chlo, I've had boyfriends before, if you'll recall." So it had been a while ago, but I'd definitely had boyfriends and gone on dates. She'd never acted this way before.

"I know you've had boyfriends. But this one is…different. He's different. There's a fire between you two."

"Chemistry," I said.

"Right. Chemistry. I mean, I saw it at the bar, but it's even more obvious now. Like, if I wasn't here, you two would shoot towards each

other like magnets and be stuck together forever." That was quite a humorous visual and I almost laughed.

"It scares me, okay?" She looked down at the floor and her voice got soft, which was rare. Usually Chloe's emotions were bright and loud and you knew what she was feeling. But this was something more vulnerable.

"You're afraid to lose me?" I sat down next to her and put my head on her shoulder.

"No," she said in a tone that told me she really meant "yes."

"How would you lose me? Am I not allowed to have a man and a best friend in my life? Is there not enough of me to go around?" She sighed and laid back on my bed, and I followed her movement so we were both staring up at my ceiling.

I hoped Fin was okay all alone in my living room.

"You know what happens when girls get boyfriends. It's inevitable. They end up spending less time with their friends and more time with the guy. I'm being completely and totally selfish, but I don't care. I'm a wreck without you, Mari. Look at how everything went down with Harmony. I don't know if I would have made it through without you. You're my port in a storm." She sniffled, and I handed her a tissue from the box on my nightstand and snuggled closer to her.

She had been an absolute mess when Harmony turned out to be the bitch that I thought she was all along. I'd never told Chloe that I had a bad feeling about her from the first day, and I wasn't going to say anything about it now.

"You would have made it, I promise. You're so much stronger than you give yourself credit for. And don't forget, I will always love you. No guy is going to come between that, and if he tries, he's an asshole and I'll get rid of him. So don't worry about losing me. I'm not going anywhere." I rubbed her shoulder and she blew her nose and tossed the tissue in my wastebasket.

"If you tell anyone I had this little breakdown, I'll kill you." Chloe often threatened me as a form of showing endearment. I was so used to it by now that if she didn't threaten me, I would have been worried.

"I wouldn't dream of it."

"Good." She sniffed again and I gave her a big hug before we both walked back into the living room to find Fin sipping wine and humming to himself.

"Everything okay?" he asked.

"Okay enough," Chloe said. "See you later." She gave both of us a little wave as she grabbed the wine bottle and moseyed out the door.

"You sure everything is okay?" he asked as I went and sat down on the couch, patting the spot next to me.

"Just a best friend thing."

Chapter
Nine

Once Chloe was gone, I didn't know what to say, or what to do. There were these moments when it hit me how successful and gorgeous he was, and I felt like a total low class frump that had nothing in common with him. It was ridiculous, but I couldn't help feeling that way. So I did the only logical thing. I got up from the couch and started cleaning the kitchen. It didn't need cleaning, but I pretended.

I heard him get up and come and stand behind me.

"What are you doing?" I jumped because his voice was closer than I'd thought. I backed up one step and came flush up against his front.

"Cleaning," I said, my voice coming out a little strangled.

"Looks clean already to me." Reaching around, he took the sponge from my hand and dropped it into the sink before running his hands back up my arms, pressing me into the counter.

"I'm really liking what these pants do to your legs." He breathed against my neck, and I could. Not. Move. Thoughts and words and all sorts of things were bursting in my brain and none of them made any sense. He pressed even harder against me and moved his hands down to my legs.

"I know we agreed to go slow, but that was before I saw you dressed like this. Not that you don't look beautiful all polished, but I love you all…messy and rumpled."

"So I look like crap?" My voice was a squeak as he used his hands to turn my body to face him. I almost caught my breath at the look in his eyes. There was no mistaking what they were filled with.

Dark, hot lust.

"No, you look completely vulnerable and delectable."

I definitely felt vulnerable. Not sure yet about the delectable part.

He reached behind my head and undid my hair, letting it tumble over my shoulders. He ran his hands through it. "Do you want me to go? I could, if I really tried. We could hit pause. It's up to you." The ball was in my court. Great. I liked that it was up to me.

"I…I want…" What the hell did I want? Him, that was for sure. Every cell of mine was drawn to him. That didn't mean it was a good choice. I always thought about my decisions. Considered every angle, made pro and con lists. There wasn't really time for that right now.

"Sweet Marisol, I can see you fighting a battle in your head. Why don't you talk it out with me?"

"Talk it out? With you?" How absurd.

"It might help you make your decision." He stepped away from me, but took my hand and led me back to the couch. I sat down on one end, and he sat on the other.

"What are the reasons you want me to stay?" I swallowed a few times before I answered.

"Because I'm attracted to you. Very much. You're interesting, and I love the way you look at me, and I think we have something between us that's worth exploring." He nodded and I saw him try and hide a goofy grin.

"Okay, and what are the reasons to not ask me to stay?" These were harder to say out loud.

"Because I don't know you. Because you're basically a stranger. Because something could happen that I might regret. Because I have no idea if you've been tested for STDs. Because my mother would be ashamed of me. Because I'm not the girl who sleeps with the guy she's just met. Because sometimes you scare me. Because of that thing you said when you left about doing things that would make my skin crawl. Because I'm scared you'll hurt me. Because I'm scared I'll fall for you." The words rushed from my mouth, the water from a punctured hose, spraying everywhere. I hadn't meant to tell him half of those things, but they came out anyway.

He leaned forward and braced his forearms on his knees, and was silent for so long I wondered where he'd gone in his head.

"Those are all valid reasons. And I know you're scared of me. I'm scared of you, too. I'm scared of what I might do to you. I'm a dark person, Marisol. I don't want to drag you down here with me." It was so hard to believe, those words he said about being dark. How could a dark person bring me a sweet present and make me laugh? How could I be attracted to someone like that?

"How would you hurt me?"

He finally looked up. "Because there are things I want to do to you, and with you, that I don't think you'd want me to. That you wouldn't be ready for. As I said, I've done things that would make your skin crawl." Now I was getting the picture of what he was talking about. What his "darkness" was. It made my heart pound and my stomach flip over.

"It seems like you've made your decision, so I'll leave now. I understand if you don't want to see me again. I won't contact you. I promise you this time. Goodbye, Marisol." He got up and headed toward the door. I had only a few seconds to make my decision.

"Wait. Don't go."

My head told me I was insane. That this was a bad idea. That he was wrong for me, no good for me, dangerous for me.

But all those thoughts went away when I saw his face as he turned back around.

"Are you sure? Because there will be no going back. This is your decision. I will respect it." His eyes were completely unreadable. I could tell he was trying not to influence my decision. Oh, but he did. If he wasn't here, in the flesh, saying no to him would be a hell of a lot easier.

I probably still wouldn't be able to.

"Stay. Please."

He exhaled slowly. "Okay."

Be careful what you ask for.

Once Fin decided he was going to stay, I had no idea what to do. With him or me.

"I'm all yours. Do what you will, Marisol. I'm yours to command." He came back over and sat on the couch, a smile playing on his lips. He was definitely pleased that I'd asked him to stay. It was a shift from the guy he'd been a few minutes ago. He was hard to keep up with.

"Oh, it's up to me, is it? And you'll do whatever I want?"

He nodded slowly. "Whatever you want."

I tapped my chin and got up from the couch, walking until I was standing behind him. "I've never been in this predicament before. The mind reels with possibilities." I leaned down until my head was right next to his. He turned to the side so we were almost face-to-face.

"You should know that I don't give up control easily. So be careful with this newfound power. It might go to your lovely head."

"Absolute power corrupts absolutely," I said, moving my mouth toward his.

"Correct," he said before I kissed him. I hadn't really decided what was going to happen. I was going to start with kissing and see where it went. I wasn't going to take anything off the table. But if we just made out and cuddled on the couch, that would be fine. If more happened? I'd have to reevaluate when we got there. If I had enough brain cells that weren't otherwise occupied.

Fin pulled away from my mouth and I looked at him in surprise.

"I'm clean, by the way. Just went to the doctor a week ago. In case you were worried." I'd sort of forgotten about it, which was probably not a good thing. I'd never really had to think about it since most of the guys I'd been with I'd known for a long time and dealt with that part long before sex was ever on the table. Tonight, everything was on the table.

I shivered in anticipation and something leaped in my chest, eager to be set free.

"Thank you for that. I appreciate it. I'm okay too. In case you were wondering." I'd had a physical six months ago and hadn't been with anyone since. Ouch. It hurt to think about how long it had been. Would I even still know what to do?

I didn't know how many women Fin had been with. I didn't even want to ask. I didn't want to know. Why was I thinking about this? I didn't want to be analyzing this decision.

So I went back to kissing him. I tried to start slow, but before I knew it, I was climbing over the back of the couch and into his lap. Our mouths began the give and take, our hands searching and reaching and caressing. We were still learning about each other. Testing and teasing. I found he liked it when I sucked on his bottom lip. He found that I liked when he tugged on my hair a little.

The kiss grew more frantic, more demanding. So did our hands. They started worrying at our clothing, which was now a nuisance. Fin's hands moved from my head to the hem of my shirt, sliding underneath and making my skin burst into goosebumps. It had actually been a good idea to go braless. It meant that there was nothing standing in the way of his hands and my breasts. Sloane would be pissed at me.

He hesitated for a brief moment before pushing his hands all the way under my shirt and upward.

"Mmm," he hummed against my lips as his fingers found my nipples. Then it was my turn to moan as he pinched them between his fingers. I arched against his hands, pulling back from the kiss.

He pinched my nipples again, but harder this time, actually digging in his fingernails a bit. It was a bright burst of pain, but I gasped in pleasure and looked down at him.

"Do you like that?" he said, his eyes lust-clouded again. He pinched again and I pushed closer to him. Yes, I definitely liked it.

Every guy I'd been with—and the list was short—had been pretty vanilla. Nothing too exciting, nothing too unusual. Most of the time I faked it so I could just go to sleep. Sex had never been all that exciting for me. I'd thought maybe there was something wrong with me, but it appeared it was just the guys. Or maybe it was the combination of me and the guys. They didn't know how to push my buttons.

But Fin. Oh, Fin.

He was pushing buttons I didn't even know I had. With him I felt…fierce. Seductive. Wild. Ready to throw him down on my floor and tear his clothes off, buttons flying everywhere. I wanted my legs in the air, his head between them, and my voice moaning his name.

I wanted him. Right now. I didn't care about anything else. If the apartment caught fire, I wouldn't leave until we were done.

Grabbing his shirt, I tried to pour everything into my kiss as he lifted my shirt over my head, exposing my top half.

He stared at me for a moment, drinking me in. I wished I could capture that look and save it. Keep it in a jar by my bedside, and whenever I was feeling unsexy or frumpy or fat, I could take it out and relive it.

He opened his mouth to say something but then closed it, instead moving his head forward until it rested between my breasts. He inhaled deeply and then looked up at me.

I had never been more naked than I was in that very moment.

"You are so lovely."

I believed him. And he was pretty lovely with his lips red and swollen from our violent kisses, and his hair in disarray from my fingers. I also realized that I was without my shirt, but he still had his on.

I ran my hands through his hair, down his neck and to his shirt, where I started working on the buttons.

"No," he said, holding my hands to stop me. "I want to keep my shirt on." His voice had a little bit of an edge to it that it hadn't a moment before.

I looked at him, confused as he took my hands and moved them so they were around his neck, before dipping his head and taking one of my nipples into his mouth, sucking hard. Hadn't he said I was the one in control?

That was one way to get me to stop trying to take his shirt off. He bit down a little, and like with his fingernails, that little nip of pain made me moan again. How had no guy ever tried this on me before?

"Do you like that?" he asked, blowing on my erect nipple.

"Yes," I said as he moved to give the other nipple the same treatment. Energy and power coiled inside me, concentrating before flowing out to my limbs and my fingers and my toes like liquid fire.

Fin kissed down my stomach and started to push down on the waistband of my pants.

Hold on. I wasn't getting naked when he hadn't even taken his shirt or shoes off. I went for his buttons again.

"No, Marisol. Don't make me ask you again." His voice was dark and commanding. I'd never heard it like that. He looked up at me and his eyes were just as serious. Was this what he meant?

"This why I told you I would ruin you. Because when I'm with you like this, I'm in control. This is how it has to be. I can't be any other way than I am. I know I said you were in control, but I can't do things that way. I'm sorry."

I opened my mouth to say something, but I didn't know what to say. This was another one of those moments when he'd changed. Changed into someone I didn't know how to deal with. What to say, what to do. I was completely thrown off balance, and now I had to struggle to catch my breath.

"Do you understand? Yes or no?" Could I do this? Could I let myself be vulnerable with him this way?

"Why?" I couldn't stop myself from asking the question. As someone who had no particular sexual preferences or desires, other than that my partner be male and have a penis, I guessed I'd never really explored or experimented.

Chloe always teased me that that's what my slutty college years were for, but since I was technically still in college, I still had a chance.

Was this my chance? My chance to take a risk, to take a chance?

"Why do I need control? That is a long story and I'm not sure if I'm ready to share it. Can you do this with me? I promise I will make it worth your while." Finally, I got a smile.

It was a possessive smile. A wolfish smile.

"What happens if I want to stop?" I definitely needed a way out. Just in case.

"You'd like to have a safeword. Naturally. Pick one and only use it if you want me to stop. Make sure it's a word you wouldn't normally say during sex." He had clearly done this before. I tried not to think about how many times and with whom. This was what he'd warned me about.

"Have you chosen your safeword?" I was trying to think of one while simultaneously trying not to notice that I was completely topless and straddling a man I'd known for less than a week.

"I'm thinking," I said. "You should have told me about this a few hours ago. I can't just come up with one on the spot."

He stared at me.

"What?"

"Nothing, just…" And he buried his face in my chest again, his body shaking. What was happening? Then a sound escaped.

"Are you laughing?"

He lifted his head and there was the goofy guy who had handed me a rubber duck. My apprehension about giving myself to him sexually lessened a bit.

"This is not a laughing matter. This is serious. I have to pick the right safeword. It's an important thing," I said.

"And what would you know about safewords, sweet Marisol?" His hands moved up and pinched my nipples again. He was trying to distract me.

"Maybe I'm not as sweet as you think I am?" In truth, Chloe had lent me a popular romance novel that had mentioned them.

"Oh no, I think you're every bit as sweet as I think you are. Maybe even sweeter. Ripe for the plucking." Did I want to be plucked? I was supposed to be deciding on my safeword. I looked around my apartment for inspiration and my eyes found the bottle with the lilacs in it.

"Lilac," I said.

"Lilac is your safeword."

"Yes."

He smiled again. "Excellent choice. Do you understand that you can use that word anytime I push you too far? And that you're not scared to use it with me?"

"I understand."

"Good. Now. I'm going to undress you." He moved me off his lap and laid me on the couch next to him before turning and lying across me.

"I could take you in the bedroom, but I want you here. So I'm going to take you here." I nodded, my breath coming quick again.

He slid down my body and started pulling my leggings down. I watched his face as he uncovered me, pulling down my underwear with the leggings until I was completely exposed.

"I love a natural girl," he said. Rory had tried to talk me into getting waxed, but I was uncomfortable about a woman I didn't know going near my vagina with hot wax.

Fin removed my leggings and tossed them aside. I shivered, but not because I was cold. I was waiting. For what, I didn't know.

He moved back up to my mouth and smoothed back my hair.

"I'm going to make sure you enjoy this. Promise." He kissed my forehead so softly, then the tip of my nose, both cheeks, my chin, and then the corners of my lips. It was terribly frustrating.

"This is all part of it, Marisol. The anticipation."

Sure, okay. I tried to be patient as he gave me feather-light kisses on my lips, pulling away as soon as I tried to kiss him back.

"Stop that," he said sharply, and my eyes flew open. The guy who had laughed at my safeword deliberation was gone again. He moved away from my lips, to my neck where he nipped and sucked his way down to my collarbone. I pushed against him, moving my hands up the back of his head to his hair, twisting it around my fingers.

"Since this is your first time, I'll go easy on you. But usually I don't allow women to touch me unless I say so." What? Was he serious?

"Why?"

"Don't ask questions," he snapped before kissing between my breasts and going back to my nipples. That was definitely the surest way to shut me up. As his mouth worked my upper half, one of his hands skimmed lower, moving between my thighs.

"You might be sweet, but you definitely want this. I can feel how wet you are already." His thumb rubbed my clit while his other fingers plunged inside me.

I gasped in surprise as his fingers filled me.

"Don't worry, I'll get you ready. You'll be screaming my name before I come inside you. And I will come inside you. Understand?"

"Yes." I was lost in a haze as his mouth and hand worked. I squirmed, wanting something, but not knowing what.

Release. Something was building in me, and if it didn't let go, I was going to die from it. Maybe that was dramatic, but I couldn't put it any other way.

He moved his fingers in and out of me, picking up the pace before he slowed again and removed his fingers. "You see that?" He held his fingers up and they glistened with wetness.

"Yes."

"Taste yourself." He pushed his fingers into my mouth. I was falling apart and lost and I didn't even know who I was anymore.

He moved me down the couch, and then settled his head between my thighs and licked me up and down in one long stroke.

My legs shook and everything inside me pulsed with want.

"You will not come yet. You will come when I say so, and I'll know if you try to lie to me."

How the hell was I supposed to do that? I couldn't control when it happened. At least, I'd never tried. I couldn't just orgasm on command. "What if I can't?" I asked, even though I knew questions were probably prohibited.

"You will. Stop asking questions." He smacked me lightly on the inside of my thigh. Was that going to be part of it? I didn't know if I was ready for *that*.

If I wanted, I could use my safeword and this would end. He'd leave, and I'd go to bed, and whenever one of my friends asked about Fin, I'd tell them that it didn't work out. He might be in charge, but I had the power to make him stop. As if he sensed my hesitation, he looked up at me as he slowly kissed my clit.

My back arched into his mouth and I was lost again.

Fin went back to work, kissing and licking with his tongue, but then he added his hand, plunging inside me with three fingers. I felt stretched, but not uncomfortable.

I was inches away from a violent orgasm.

"Not yet. I told you, not yet. Not until I say," he growled, thrusting harder with his fingers.

"I can't help it," I panted, trying to get control of my body. It didn't want to be controlled.

That earned me another smack, and somehow that loosed my orgasm. I cried out, but he clamped his hand over my mouth.

"I told you not yet." He was angry. Really angry. He'd gone all the way to the level of pissed.

As I came down from my orgasm, he continued to stare at me, searching for something.

The anger melted from his eyes and he pushed himself away from me with so much force, he almost fell of the couch. "I'm sorry. I can't."

What?

I pushed myself up on my elbows, still in a post-orgasmic haze. He was the one who'd initiated this, who'd told me what he wanted.

Granted, I hadn't really followed his rules, but this was my first time. I wasn't going to be perfect.

"Why?"

He grabbed his coat and shoved his arm through one of the sleeves, but didn't bother to do the other. It was a replay from just the other night, when he'd bolted.

Fin backed away from me like I'd just developed a highly contagious disease. "I can't do this with you. Not now, not ever. Goodbye, Marisol. I'm so, so sorry."

And before I could throw my clothes on, he was slamming my door.

She was absolutely lovely. Lovely in a way that she was completely unaware of which only made it worse. Add that to the fact she seemed completely captivated by me, and it was all I could do not to take her hand and drag her out of the smoky bar.

But I couldn't do what I wanted with this girl. She was Rory's friend, and she was innocent. No, she wasn't a virgin (that I knew of), but she definitely hadn't experienced the kind of sex that I would want to have with her. It would change her. It had changed me.

Listening to her voice bubble out of her sweet mouth and see her eyes flash when she talked about her graduate studies made me wish I was passionate about something. Well, something other than fucking and obsessively collecting books wherever I went.

"I'm so sorry, I've been talking your ear off," she said, fiddling with one of her earrings. It was dark, but I could still see the blush that spread on her cheeks.

"It's okay, I don't mind." She could talk to me about paint drying and I'd listen. She laughed nervously and licked her lips. I wanted to taste those lips. I wanted to do a lot of things with those lips. No, I couldn't think of her that way. She wasn't that kind of girl. Marisol was the kind of girl my mother would want me to marry. Sweet. Compliant. Would look the other way when I inevitably strayed from my wedding vows and sought an outlet for my "depravity." Just like my father did with my mother.

I didn't want to think about my father. Thinking about him made me have dark thoughts, and those dark thoughts led to dark desires. I was going to have to visit Sapphire before my trip was out. Of all the women I'd been with, she always seemed to know what I wanted and how to give it to me. Plus, she always seemed to know when I was coming and had a room at her club ready for me. She was worth every cent.

"So, what about you?" Marisol asked, invading my thoughts of Sapphire. She gripped her drink, twisting it back and forth.

"What about me, Marisol?" I couldn't get enough of her name. I loved the way it tasted in my mouth, and the little smile she got whenever I used it.

"Well, all I know about you is what Rory has told me."

"Oh, I'm sure everything was complimentary." I shot Rory a look across the table, but she was too busy being enthralled by Mr. Lucas Blaine. He wasn't the kind of fellow I'd pictured her with but the chemistry between the two of them was undeniable.

"She might have told me a few stories about the two of you getting into trouble when you were younger." Sometimes I forgot that Rory had dirt on me from my distant past. Thankfully we hadn't stayed in touch recently, and she was completely unaware of what I'd become.

I smiled at Marisol and shifted closer to her to gauge her reaction. She leaned closer to me and dropped her voice. "Well, from what she said, you got into a lot of trouble." If only she knew.

"Sometimes I did. Sometimes I was able to talk my way out of it." I couldn't take my eyes off her lips.

"Oh, I bet you did." She laughed softly.

We talked for a while longer about mundane things. Silly, unimportant things. Rory and Mr. Lucas Blaine made their exit, followed by Sloane, and then it was just me, Marisol, and Chloe, who was radiating protective energy at me. She didn't have to worry. I wasn't going to do anything with Marisol. I was going to be charming and take her on dates and pay for dinner and open doors and be a perfect gentleman. Plus, I could flirt mercilessly with her, which would be highly entertaining. Maybe even better than sex. Verbal intercourse was highly underrated, in my opinion.

I could do this. I'd date Marisol and flirt with her and that would be enough. It had to be enough. I couldn't take this sweet girl by the hand and lead her down the path that I'd chosen to follow. A path littered with shadows and gnarled trees that were covered in thorns that would tear her apart slowly and reduce her to nothing.

I would not let that happen. If I took things too far, pushed too hard, then I would bow out. Leave. Push her away to keep her intact. I would not wreck this one.

"It's getting late," Marisol said, glancing at her phone. "I should probably call it a night." She shifted, as if she knew that she should go but didn't want to. I didn't want her to go either. Well, I wanted her to go, but I wanted to be going with her.

"You're right. But I would definitely like to see you again." She smiled and grabbed my phone where it rested on the table, typed something in and then handed it back to me.

"There. Now you have my number. What's yours?" I gave it to her and she put it in her phone.

"Well, goodnight, Fin Herald," she said, getting up from the stool. "It was nice to meet you."

"It was lovely to meet you, Marisol."

And coming April 17

Deep Surrendering

(Episode 2) . . .

A word about this novella:

Deep Surrendering is a series of novellas that tell the story of Fin and Marisol. Each novella is around 20,000 words and contains a complete story, but all are part of a larger story arc. They will be released on the third Thursday of each month. The number of episodes is still being decided, but it will be around 12-14, which is two complete novel's worth of content. For news about this series, please check out chelseamcameron.com and sign up for Chelsea's newsletter.

Thank You

I thought that writing a short novel would be a piece of cake. Whatever that means. In fact, this has been one of the hardest projects I've worked on. I owe a debt of gratitude first to Jen, my editor, Kara, my copyeditor and Laura, my beta reader ninja, who weren't afraid to tell me what parts worked and what didn't. I couldn't have done this without you. Thanks also go to my family and friends, my author community, my formatter, Ali, and to YOU for taking this new journey with me. I promise it will be worth it in the end, but we're going to hit a bit of turbulence first. You ready for the ride?

Books by
Chelsea

The Noctalis Chronicles

Nocturnal (Book One)
Nightmare (Book Two)
Neither (Book Three)
Neverend (Book Four)

The Whisper Trilogy

Whisper (Book One)

Fall and Rise

Deeper We Fall (Book One)
Faster We Burn (Book Two)

My Favorite Mistake
(Available from Harlequin)

Surrendering

Sweet Surrendering
Surrendering to Us

For Real

My Sweetest Escape (January 28, 2014)

About Chelsea

Chelsea M. Cameron is a YA/NA New York Times/USA Today Best Selling author from Maine. Lover of things random and ridiculous, Jane Austen/Charlotte and Emily Bronte Fangirl, red velvet cake enthusiast, obsessive tea drinker, vegetarian, former cheerleader and world's worst video gamer. When not writing, she enjoys watching infomercials, singing in the car and tweeting. She has a degree in journalism from the University of Maine, Orono that she promptly abandoned to write about the people in her own head. More often than not, these people turn out to be just as weird as she is.

Find Chelsea online:

chelseamcameron.com
Twitter: @chel_c_cam
Facebook: Chelsea M. Cameron (Official Author Page)

Made in the USA
Charleston, SC
15 March 2014